# Lili at Ballet

## Rachel Isadora

Methuen Children's Books

First published in Great Britain in 1993
by Methuen Children's Books
an imprint of Reed Consumer Books Limited
Michelin House, 81 Fulham Road, London SW3 6RB
and Auckland, Melbourne, Singapore and Toronto

Designed by Nanette Stevenson
Hand-lettering by David Gatti

0 416 18941 5

Produced by Mandarin Offset

Printed and bound in China

For Gillian

This is Lili. She dreams of becoming a ballerina. Sometimes she dances at home with her cat, Pandora.

When Lili saw the ballet *Giselle* with her dance class, she wanted to practise even harder. She knows there will be many years of hard work ahead before she can join a ballet company.

long-sleeved
leotard

sleeveless
leotard

tights

short
practice tutu

tutu
with bodice

Lili has ballet lessons four afternoons a week. Everyone wears clothes made just for dancing. Lili tries on a long practice tutu.

ballet
slippers

pointe
shoes

footless
tights

socks

T-shirt

leg
warmers

She thinks about being the flower fairy
in the school performance at the end of
the year.

Students get ready for class in the dressing rooms. They change into leotards and tights. Some put up their hair. Others work on their homework or sew elastic on to their ballet slippers.

Lili likes dancing to classical music played on the piano. The mirrors show the students how their steps look. They hold onto the barre for balance.

bending forward
to stretch back
and legs

lunging forward
to arch back
and stretch legs

stretching on the floor
to turn out the hips
and arch the back

Students do warm-up stretches and bends before class. These
exercises make their muscles more supple.

feet touching,
knees turned out
to turn out the legs

backbend to stretch
back and arms

side split to stretch legs
and back and turn out the legs

Here is Lili's teacher, Madame Popova. The first exercise begins
at the barre. Madame Popova tells Nanette to pull in her tummy
and reminds the class to turn out their feet.

grand pas de chat
développé

jeté

These are some of the ballet steps. Ballet began in France about
300 years ago, and the steps are still called by their French names.

passé
en pointe

changement
en l'air

attitude

arabesque

first position                    second position

After the barre work is finished, the students move to the centre
of the floor.  They practise the five classical positions.  Now they
must balance on their own.

third position          fourth position          fifth position

During the last part of class, Madame Popova asks the students to combine steps and dance across the floor. These are called *combinations*. The students leap and turn, using the whole studio space. Lili likes this part of class best.

Lili has seen ballerinas on stage dance on their toes, or *sur les pointes*. When she is older and her feet are stronger, she will begin practising *en pointe*, too.

Girls begin to go en pointe around the age of eleven. They wear their pointe shoes for a few minutes at the end of their ballet class.
As their bones and muscles strengthen they will wear their pointe shoes for longer periods of time and do more difficult steps.

Shank: a stiff support for the arch, in the sole of the shoe

Drawstring tightens the shoe around the foot.

Vamp: the upper part of the front of the shoe

Box: the entire front of the shoe, most of which is stiff

Satin ribbons tie around the ankle for support.

Rosin box:
rosin is used
to prevent
slipping

Most students wear
pink satin pointe
shoes for class.

Pointe shoes are
sometimes dyed different
colours to match the
ballerina's costumes.

"stag" jeté

croisé derrière

There is also a special class just for boys. They practise jumping
high and turning fast.

pas de poisson

grand pas de chat
développé

Lili can't wait until she's old enough for the *variations* class.
There she'll learn roles from different ballets and perform them
in recital. Lili's class has been practising to be flowers in their
student performance.

Candy Cane from
"The Nutcracker"

The White Cat and
Puss in Boots
from "The Sleeping Beauty"

Odette from
"Swan Lake"

Albrecht and Giselle
from "Giselle"

Firebird from
"The Firebird"

Petroushka from
"Petroushka"

When the night of the school performance arrives, Lili dances the part of the flower fairy. She waves her wand and the flowers begin to dance.

Backstage, after the performance, Lili still feels like the flower fairy.
She waves her wand, smiles, and makes a secret wish.